Nella
THE
PRINCESS KNIGHT

Based on the television series created by **Christine Ricci**
Illustrated by **Alessandra Sorrentino**

Random House 🏠 **New York**

randomhousekids.com

ISBN 978-1-5247-18756

Printed in the United States of America

10 9 8 7 6 5 4 3 2 1

Once there was a beautiful princess who lived in the kingdom of Castlehaven. Princess Nella loved attending royal balls and fancy picnics in her glitzy gowns, sparkling crowns, and shiny shoes. But she also dreamed of other things.

From her balcony, Princess Nella could see beyond the kingdom walls.

I wonder what it would be like to climb mountains, camp in caves, and discover wild creatures, she thought. *I wish I were a daring and courageous knight.*

One day, Princess Nella was walking in the royal garden when she spotted a small gate hidden behind the rosebushes. She pushed it open and stepped into . . .

. . . the Dragon Blossom Woods!

The creatures there were very friendly.
A cute little chipsqueak landed on Princess Nella's
arm and chirped hello. A bouncy, flop-eared fleagle
brought her a flower.

"If I am very quiet," whispered Nella, "maybe
a critterdragon will land on my finger!"

Just then, Nella heard a
soft whimper. She followed the
sound and discovered a unicorn
stuck in a bog!
　"Help!" cried the unicorn.
"This bog goop is ruining my
new ruby horseshoes!"
　Nella quickly pulled the unicorn
out of the muck.

The unicorn's mane was quite
goopy, so Nella invited her to rinse off
in a bubble bath back at the castle.

The unicorn giggled. "A royal bathtub
filled with glittery bubbles? That's a
unicorn's dream!"

Princess Nella was curious about her new friend.

"What's your name?" she asked.

"Trinket," replied the unicorn.

"That's a perfect name for you," said Nella,
"because trinkets are unique, beautiful,
and very special, just like you."

Trinket's horn glowed bright with happiness.

Then Trinket handed Nella a present: a special stone called the Knightly Heart. It twinkled in Nella's hand.

"It's beautiful," she said.

Trinket smiled. "It's also magical. Friendship makes the Knightly Heart grow stronger, and kindness makes it sparkle. And when you need it most, it will give you courage!"

Trinket and Nella became the best of friends. Trinket even moved in to the stable next door to the castle!

One night, Trinket and Nella were having a fancy and frilly campout. As they snuggled into their sleeping bags, a dark shadow crossed the moon.

An enormous dragon scooped
Trinket up, sleeping bag and all, and
flew off toward Snowburst Peak!
"Oh, no! Trinket is in danger!"
cried Nella. "I've got to rescue her!"

Princess Nella felt lost and scared among
the tall trees and majestic mountains.
*If only I were as daring and courageous as
a knight,* she thought as she clutched
her heart-shaped stone tightly.

While Nella was on her way to save Trinket, a gust of wind blew a chipsqueak nest out of its tree. She raced to catch it. She used a ribbon to weave the nest together and tie it to a branch.

The thankful chipsqueaks flew alongside her, keeping her company on the way to Snowburst Peak. When she got deeper into the forest, Nella pulled a flop-eared fleagle out of a thorny bush. She even shared a snack with a hungry giant!

Soon all kinds of critters and creatures had joined Nella's journey, and with each new friendship, she felt a bit braver and the Knightly Heart glowed a bit brighter.

Not far from Snowburst Peak, Princess Nella and her new friends came upon an enchanted labyrinth.

Inside, a Bafflin was caught in some vines.
Princess Nella gently untangled her.

The Bafflin was so grateful that she
offered to fly Nella to the dragon's cave!

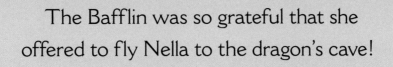

Nella could hear strange sounds
coming from inside the cave. She stopped
and took out the Knightly Heart.
"I have always dreamed of doing great
things," she said. "And now I know
that the greatest thing I can do is
help a friend."

Suddenly, the heart began to
SPARKLE!

As the magical heart grew more and more powerful, Nella realized that being a princess was only *part* of who she was. She was also a kind and caring friend, and that made her as daring and courageous as a knight.

"MY HEART IS BRIGHT! I AM A PRINCESS KNIGHT!"

Sparkles burst from the heart, swirling and whirling around Nella's gown and transforming it into a dazzling suit of armor! Her tiara flipped over and became the handle of a glowing sword!

Feeling stronger and braver than
ever before, Nella spotted the dragon's
shadow cast across an icy crevice!

"To cross that crevice,
I'm going to need a net!"
Nella exclaimed. She tossed
her sword into the air, and
as it twirled, it turned into
a gleaming archer's bow.

Nella launched several ribbon arrows across the
crevice, and they weaved together to form a bridge.
She bravely climbed onto the bridge and crossed over.

"I'm coming, Trinket!" shouted Nella as she expanded her shield into a glistening snowboard.

Carving into each turn, she sailed over the snowy jumps and bumps. She picked up speed as her board soared across the snow.

Finally, she landed in a spray of ice crystals
right in front of the dragon!

Summoning all her knightly
courage, Nella told the dragon, "I'm
here to rescue my unicorn friend!"
Then she grabbed the sleeping
bag, opened it, and released Trinket.
"You're my dazzling hero!"
said Trinket, and she gave Nella
the best unicorn hug ever!

The dragon was surprised!
"Huh? I didn't know a
unicorn was in there," she
said. "I only wanted a
blanket because my cave
is so cold and dreary."

"This calls for a dragon cave makeover!" exclaimed Nella.

"Yes!" cheered Trinket. "Looks like a courageous princess knight and her very fashionable unicorn have some work to do!"

Soon Nella and Trinket had turned the dragon's lonely ice cave into a bright, cozy home filled with flowers and friends!

Back at her own home, Nella and Trinket made
a necklace with the Knightly Heart so Nella could
wear it every day.

"I love being both a dazzling princess and a
courageous knight," said Nella proudly. "But helping
friends is what really makes my heart sparkle!"